STELLA

FAIRY OF THE FOREST

MARIE-LOUISE GAY

A GROUNDWOOD BOOK   DOUGLAS & McINTYRE   TORONTO VANCOUVER BUFFALO

Groundwood Books / Douglas & McIntyre Ltd.
720 Bathurst Street, Suite 500, Toronto, Ontario M5S 2R4

Distributed in the U.S.A. by Publishers Group West
1700 Fourth Street, Berkeley, CA 94710

We acknowledge the financial support of the Canada Council for the Arts, the Ontario
Arts Council and the Government of Canada through the Book Publishing Industry
Development Program for our publishing activities.

ONTARIO ARTS COUNCIL
CONSEIL DES ARTS DE L'ONTARIO

National Library of Canada Cataloguing in Publication Data
Gay, Marie-Louise
Stella, fairy of the forest
"A Groundwood book".
ISBN 0-88899-448-6 (bound).– ISBN 0-88899-598-9 (pbk)
I. Title.
PS8563.A868S732 2002   jC813'.54   C2001-930756-X
PZ7.G38St 2002

Printed and bound in China

To my father

"Stella!" called Sam. "Stella! Where are you?"
"Here," whispered Stella.

"Where?" said Sam. "I can't see you."
"That's because I'm practicing to be invisible," said Stella.

"Now I see you," said Sam. "How did you do that?"
"I thought of invisible things," answered Stella, "like wind or music…"
"Or fairies?" asked Sam.

"Fairies aren't invisible," said Stella. "I've seen hundreds of them."
"Really?" said Sam. "Where did you see them?".
"In the forest," said Stella. "Over there. Let's go, Sam."

"I don't know," said Sam. "Are there any bears in the forest?"
"Bears sleep during the day," said Stella. "Come on, Sam."

"What do fairies look like?" asked Sam.
"They're tiny and beautiful," said Stella, "and they fly very fast."
"I see one!" said Sam. "Look!"

"That's a butterfly, Sam," said Stella.
"Do butterflies eat butter?" asked Sam.
"Yellow butterflies do," said Stella.

"Then I guess blue butterflies eat pieces of sky," said Sam.
"How do you know that?" asked Stella.
"I know a lot of things," said Sam.

"Look," said Sam, "some clouds just landed in that field."
"Those aren't clouds, Sam. They're sheep."
"Aren't sheep dangerous?" asked Sam.

"About as dangerous as woolly blankets," said Stella.
"Let's go say hello to them."
"You go," said Sam. "I'll just wave."

"Who planted all these flowers?" asked Sam.
"The birds and the bees," said Stella.
"Bees!" cried Sam. "Won't they sting us?"

"Not if you move ve-r-r-y slowly," said Stella.
"Stella?" said Sam. "You have a bee in your hair."
"Run, Sam, run!" cried Stella.

"We have to cross the stream," said Stella.
"I don't want to get my feet wet," said Sam.
"I'll carry you. Hop on!"

"Isn't it too slippery?" asked Sam. "Won't we fall in?"
"No, we won't," said Stella. "I'll walk on these rocks."
"Stella?" said Sam. "One of the rocks is moving."

"No, it isn't, Sam."
"Uh-oh…" said Sam.

"Was that a turtle, Stella?" asked Sam.
"Yes, Sam," sighed Stella.

"Isn't the forest beautiful?" said Stella. "Look at these big old trees."
"Are they older than Grandma?" asked Sam.
"Almost," said Stella. "They must be at least a hundred years old."

"Is that why their skin is so wrinkled?" asked Sam.
"That's not skin," said Stella. "That's bark."
"Grandma's bark is much softer," said Sam. "Especially on her cheeks."

"Climb up here, Sam," said Stella. "You can see the whole world."
"Can rabbits climb trees?" asked Sam.

"No, but you can," said Stella. "Come on, Sam. It's lovely up here."
"It's lovely down here, too," said Sam. "With the rabbits."

"Look, Sam," said Stella. "Isn't this a pretty snake?"
"It's pretty long," said Sam. "Don't snakes swallow people?"
"It's too small," said Stella.

"Maybe it only swallows small people," said Sam. "What's that?"
"A porcupine," said Stella. "Don't touch! It's very prickly."
"Why would anyone want to touch a porcupine?" said Sam. "Or a snake?"

"I'm the king of the castle," sang Stella.
"How do rocks grow so big?" asked Sam.
"A giant waters them every day," said Stella. "Come on up, Sam."

"I think the giant is watering his rocks right now," said Sam.
"It's just raining, Sam," said Stella. "Let's build a forest house."

"How?" asked Sam. "Why?"
"We'll make the roof out of branches and ferns," said Stella.
"And we'll sleep on a bed of moss."

"Sleep?" said Sam. "Won't the bears be waking up soon?"
"Just help me carry the ferns," said Stella.

"This is perfect," said Stella.

"What do we do now?" asked Sam.

"Look for fairies," said Stella. "If you see a fairy, you can make a wish."

"I see one!" cried Sam.
"Where? Where?"
"Too late!" said Sam. "It just flew away."

"Oh, well," said Stella. "What was your wish?"
"I wish I could stay here forever," said Sam.
"Me, too," said Stella.